This book belongs to

_____

"Speak the truth to one another."
Zechariah 8:16

Published by Scholastic Inc., 90 Old Sherman Turnpike, Danbury, Connecticut 06816.

ISBN: 0-7172-9844-2

Printed in the U.S.A.

First Scholastic printing, February 2006

TO BE FILED

The Slobfather

A Lesson in Telling the Truth

Written by Doug Peterson
Illustrated by Big Idea Design

SCHOLASTIC INC.
New York   Toronto   London   Auckland   Sydney
Mexico City   New Delhi   Hong Kong   Buenos Aires

Ladies and gentlemen, the story you are about to read is silly.

The names have been changed to protect the serious. My name is Larry the Cucumber, private detective, and my partner is Bob the Tomato. He carries a badge. I carry a badger. Don't ask why.

Bob and I are not your usual detectives. We look into messes, not crimes. Yeah, you heard right. Spills, clutter, trash, litter. All kinds of messes. You might say that we are mess detectives. This is our story.

1:25 p.m. My partner and I were working the day watch on the Southside of town when the call came in. Someone had a messy room in progress. So we hopped into our car and raced to 201 Bumbly Boulevard.

1:36 p.m. We rushed into the house of the Asparagus family and bolted upstairs. But we were too late. Junior Asparagus' bedroom was a total mess. It looked like a tornado had struck. No. Worse. It looked like a stampede of dizzy water buffalo had run around in circles through the room for a few hours—right before a tornado hit.

There were clothes everywhere. Toys covered every inch of the floor. Junior Asparagus, a little guy in a bright blue hat, sat in the corner, his eyes wide with shock.

"My name is Detective Larry, and this is my partner Bob," I said to Junior. "He carries a badge. I carry a badger. Don't ask why."

"What happened here, Junior?" asked Bob.
It was a good question. Why didn't I think of it?

As I pulled out my notepad, the boy's eyes darted to
the right and to the left. He looked nervous. I made
a note of that.

"It wasn't my fault!" Junior pleaded. "I didn't make this mess!"

"You didn't?" Bob said. "Then who did?"

It took a moment before Junior answered. Then his eyes brightened and words came tumbling out of his mouth.

"A bunch of gangsters broke into my room and threw all of my clothes on the floor!" Junior said. "Uh, yeah...that's right! I tried to stop them, but they just laughed and dumped out my laundry basket."

"Hmmmm, slob
mobsters," I said. "We call
them 'slobsters' in the police business.
This sounds serious."

"This sounds hard to believe," whispered Bob.

Bob was getting on my nerves. I made a note of that.

1:45 p.m. We left Junior's messy room and decided to drive back to headquarters to file our report. That's when another call came in. There was trouble again at the Asparagus home. Someone had spilled milk.

1:51 p.m. Bob and I burst through the front door of the Asparagus house. There it was. A huge puddle of milk right next to the kitchen table.

Junior stared sadly at the puddle. His mother stood next to him, talking to him about the mess.

While I drew a chalk outline around the spilled milk, Bob started asking questions. "What happened?" he asked Mom Asparagus who began telling us all about her day. "Just the facts, ma'am," Bob added.

Drat. I wish I had said that. I always wanted to say, "Just the facts, ma'am."

"I was in the other room folding clothes when I heard an awful crash," Mom Asparagus said. "So I rushed into the kitchen, and I found milk all over the floor. But Junior said he didn't do it."

I looked up from my notepad. This sounded interesting. "You didn't do it?" I said to Junior. "Then who did? Was it that gang of nasty slobsters again?"

Bob rolled his eyes. I made a note of that.

"That's right!" Junior exclaimed. "A gang of slobsters broke into our house, tipped over the milk, and ran out the back door, laughing."

I dusted for fingerprints on the back door. But Bob reminded me that veggies don't have fingers, so I checked for nose prints instead.

"This is a little far-fetched," Bob whispered to me. Then he turned to Junior and asked, "Did you get a good look at those guys?"

Junior thought and puzzled and pondered. "I think there were three of them," he said. "The leader was a big zucchini wearing sunglasses and a hat."

"Hmmmm," I said. "Sounds like the work of the Slobfather."

"The who?" said Bob.

"The Slobfather," I said. "The mastermind of messes. The kingpin of clutter. I'm surprised you never heard of him, Bob." Bob just shook his head and sighed.

2:30 p.m. Taking a break from our busy day, Bob and I decided to stop and buy a couple of blueberry slushies. But no sooner had we sat down when we were called back to the Asparagus house. A pattern was developing. I made a note of it.

2:37 p.m. I was stunned. I had never seen anything like it before in my life.

When we came back to Junior Asparagus' bedroom, all of the toys were gone. Every piece of clothing had been put away.

But there was one problem. A big problem. Something very large had been shoved underneath the rug in Junior's room. The rug had a big bump in the middle that stuck up like a mini mountain range. I should know. I tripped over it.

Junior sat on the bed, humming to himself. His father stood in the doorway, looking concerned.

"May I look under the rug?" Bob asked Dad Asparagus. Junior's father nodded.

Carefully, slowly, Bob lifted the rug. I had to turn away. I didn't have the stomach to look. It was too awful. Someone had shoved all of Junior's toys and dirty clothes underneath the rug. There was even a half-eaten box of Marshmallow Crunch cereal.

"Who would do such a thing?"
I gasped.

"The slobsters did it!" Junior insisted. "The slobsters came into my room when I was cleaning it up. And they shoved everything underneath the rug! I tried to stop them, but I couldn't."

"That's terrible," I said. "The Slobfather must be stopped!"

Bob stared at me in disbelief. "Larry, don't you get it?" he said. "There are no slob mobsters."

"Slobsters, you mean."

"There are no slobsters, Larry."

"Then who made the mess in Junior's room?" I said. "And who spilled milk in the kitchen? And who shoved everything under Junior's rug?"

"I have an idea, but I'm going to need some help," Bob said. Then he turned and looked straight at Junior. So did Dad Asparagus. And so did my badger. I thought I might as well look at Junior too. Don't ask me why.

"Junior, are you sure there isn't anything else you'd like to tell us?" asked Bob. "Isn't it time to face the truth?"

The little asparagus turned away and peered up at the ceiling. He said nothing.

"You probably thought that telling lies would get you out of this mess," said Dad Asparagus gently, sitting on the bed next to Junior. "But trying to hide the truth by lying is like trying to shove all of your things under the rug. It doesn't work. Telling lies just makes an even *bigger* mess."

"Lies hurt everyone, including the person who tells them," added Bob. "If you tell lies all the time, people will have a hard time trusting you."

I made a note of that.

"Are you *sure* you don't have something else you'd like to say?"
Bob asked Junior again.

Junior let out a big sigh. Then all of a sudden, he broke down.

"All right, all right, I did it!" he blurted. "*I* made the big mess in my room. *I* spilled the milk. And when Dad asked me to pick up my room, *I* shoved everything under the rug. It was easier than cleaning. I'm sorry! I'm really sorry!"

I never saw this coming. Junior had confessed to everything. He'd told the truth and had come clean.

You mean there were no slobsters?" I said, scribbling wildly in my notepad.

"No slobsters," admitted Junior.

"And no Slobfather?"

"No Slobfather," he said.

"Now don't you feel better?" Dad Asparagus said. "It feels good to tell the truth. God doesn't want our lives getting messed up with lies. That's worse than having a messy room."

I made a note of that.

"I'm glad I told the truth, but now everyone is mad at me," Junior admitted.

"Junior, you did what God wants by telling the truth, so I forgive you," his dad told him.

Junior's eyes went wide with surprise. "You forgive me? Does that mean I won't get punished?"

"Well, I didn't say that," Dad Asparagus smiled. "You still have to face the consequences for lying. While you clean up this mess, you'll have to miss your favorite TV show. But I still love you, and God does too."

3:15 p.m.
As we left the Asparagus house, Junior was getting big hugs from his Mom and Dad.

"So there are no slobsters," I said as I filled out the report of Case #101.

"That's right," Bob said. "When we try to cover up what we've done by lying, it can feel pretty bad inside. It's like there's a big mess deep inside us. But when we tell the truth, those messy feelings are all cleaned up."

Case closed. Tears of joy came to my eyes and I blew my nose with a mighty HONK!

"Uh…Larry?" said Bob.

"Yes, Bob."

"You just blew your nose in your notepad."

I made a note of that. Time to get a new notepad.

Detective Doodles

Every good detective notices even the smallest details. In this story, Larry writes clues in his notepad. Look at Larry's notepad doodles below and read his notes. Can you name each mystery object and find it on the pages of this story?

Look closely and you'll see, You can dust for nose prints with me.

Quack, quack, quack I say, I'm as yellow as a sunny day.

Bright red and speedy I am, zoom me around as fast as you can.

Veggie Value to Share

God asks us to tell the truth even if there are consequences. What are some reasons you think it is important to tell the truth?

Switch me on,
switch me off,
When you can't see,
look for me.

Strong is what I make
your teeth and bones,
But it's up to you to
drink me on your own.

I am a tiny, little,
shiny machine,
Be sure to give me oil
and keep me clean.

Cuddly,
brown,
and white,
I'm such a cute sight!

Tie me up
around a neck,
Am I straight?
You'd better check!

Blow, blow, blow,
The mighty wind
makes me go!